F
GIL   Gilson, Jamie.

            Itchy Richard.

                        33197000026141

$13.45

DATE		
11-29		
1-19		
4-6		
4-13		
9-19		
10-11		
10-19		
10-26		
12-21		
3-15		
4-11		
4-19		

DISCARDED

Itchy Richard

Jamie Gilson

Itchy Richard

Illustrated by Diane de Groat

Clarion Books

NEW YORK

Clarion Books
a Houghton Mifflin Company imprint
215 Park Avenue South, New York, NY 10003
Text copyright © 1991 by Jamie Gilson
Illustrations copyright © 1991 by Diane de Groat

Library of Congress Cataloging-in-Publication Data

Gilson, Jamie.
Itchy Richard / by Jamie Gilson.
p. cm.
Summary: Second graders and their teacher experience an outbreak
of head lice.
ISBN 0-395-59282-8
[1. Lice—Fiction. 2. Schools—Fiction.] I. Title.
PZ7.G4385It 1992
[Fic]—dc20   91-6567   CIP   AC

BP 10 9 8 7 6 5 4 3 2 1

For Paul Nilsen. Thanks.

Contents

∘ 1 ∘

I Need It

"Can I have four dollars?" I called to my mom. "I need it for an eyeball yo-yo."

Mom stopped brushing her teeth. "You need *what*?" she called back from the bathroom.

I stirred my Nice Day rice cereal. Lots of yellow marshmallow smiley faces were floating in the milk. I picked one out and put it on the table. It was happy.

"An eyeball yo-yo," I said, louder. "A yo-yo. You know, a thing that goes up and down on a string. I need it for school."

"Sure, Richard," Mom said, coming into the

kitchen. "I know what a yo-yo is. It's the eyeball part I don't get."

I scooped out another smiley face and put it next to the first. They both grinned at me.

"It's fun," I told her. "It looks like a big round eyeball. When it goes up and down, the eyeball rolls round and round. All the kids have one."

I picked out another yellow marshmallow and put it on the table. Three Nice Day faces smiled back at me.

"And you need this for school?" Mom asked.

"Yes," I told her, "I do."

She opened her purse.

"Richard," she asked me, "did Mrs. Zookey really tell you to bring a yo-yo eye to school?"

"I think it glows in the dark," I said. "I'm not sure, but I think so. It only costs four dollars. Plus tax."

"Four dollars is not *only*. It's a lot," Mom said, and she closed her purse.

I picked out another yellow face and set it on the table with the smile upside down. It was not happy.

"Don't play with your food," Mom said.

"Everybody else at Table Two has an eyeball

yo-yo," I told her. "I'm the only one who doesn't."

"You don't need *everything* Table Two has." She looked up at the clock. "We're late," she said.

"Ben wasn't at school yesterday," I said fast. "I bet he was at home practicing new yo-yo tricks. His eyeball is purple. He can make it do Walk the Dog down the hall."

"That's awful," Mom told me. "That's just awful."

"No, it's not. It's funny. Linda's eyeball is orange. Dawn Marie is bringing hers today. She said so. That leaves me. I'm the only kid at Table Two who doesn't have one."

"You'd better finish your breakfast," Mom said, "or we'll both miss our buses." She leaned down and gave me a hug.

"Please," I tried. "We *always* do things together at Table Two."

She put her purse strap over her shoulder. "Not *always*. Not this time. There are better things to buy with four dollars than a walking eyeball. Let's go." She opened the door.

I looked into my bowl. The smiley faces left in it were frowning at me, every one. This was not going to be a very nice day.

○ 2 ○

All Together Now

Ben's yo-yo had a big purple eye on one half. The other half was white with lots and lots of red lines like veins with blood in them. As we headed down the hall to class he made it Walk the Dog. It bounced, bounced, bounced along the floor. It rolled its eye at all the kids we passed.

"Can I try?" Yolanda asked him.

"No," he said. "It's mine."

"Let me do it," Michael said.

"No way," Ben told him. "You might break it."

"I'm getting mine tomorrow," I told them. "Mom said."

Linda met us at the door of our classroom. She

was making her big orange eyeball spin round and round like a Ferris wheel.

"It's called Around the World," she said. "It's my best trick."

"Can you do that?" I asked Ben.

"Sure," he said, but he didn't even try.

"I can, too," I told him. "Let me use yours. You can use mine tomorrow. I think I'll get a yellow one."

He didn't want to let me. I could tell. But Table Two sticks together, so he pulled the string off his finger and handed me the yo-yo.

"It's not easy," he said.

If Linda could go Around the World, so could I. I slipped the string on and held the big plastic eyeball tight.

I'd never held a yo-yo before. It was warm from Ben's hand. The red lines were raised, and I could feel them.

I lifted it up high the way Ben and Linda had and then let go. I watched as the eye slid all the way down the string to the floor. It stopped. It wouldn't come back up. I pulled and pulled, but it wouldn't come. It sat still.

Linda covered her mouth and giggled. Ben

laughed out loud, so I peeled the string off my finger and gave the yo-yo back to him. I didn't want it anymore, anyway. It didn't work.

The bell rang and the three of us sat at our places and crossed our hands. Dawn Marie was already there. Nobody at Table Two was absent.

"You weren't here yesterday," I said to Ben. "Were you sick?"

"Not really," he said. He uncrossed his hands and stuck the yo-yo in his mouth so he had three eyes.

"I like the way you're crossing your hands on your tables," Mrs. Zookey said. When she likes the way we do things, our teacher always tells us.

We like her OK. She hardly ever shouts. She wears silvery earrings that are cats playing with balls. She has lots and lots of red hair. And her eyes are green.

"Who is Teacher's Pet today?" Mrs. Zookey asked.

Yolanda, who sits at Table Three, raised her hand. Teacher's Pet gets to do all the good stuff like take attendance, go to the office with the milk count, erase the chalkboard, and lead the Pledge. There's a new Teacher's Pet every day. A list on the wall tells whose day it is.

Yolanda went to the front of the room and put her hand over her heart. We all stood up.

"I pledge. . ." she began.

Everybody was looking at the flag, even Mrs. Zookey.

Ben quick picked up his eyeball yo-yo and stuck his finger into the string loop. Then he swung the yo-yo around just like Linda had done. Just like I didn't do. Up it went and over. But it didn't keep going Around the World the way hers had. It let go.

It slipped off its string and shot out like a rocket.

Just when we got to the part about "liberty and justice for all," the yo-yo sailed across the room.

It flew by kids whose hands were on their hearts. It just missed the class lizards in their glass aquarium. It zipped past Mrs. Zookey's nose. Then it hit the chalkboard with a thwack.

When Ben's yo-yo fell to the floor, it cracked in half and rolled two ways. When it stopped, its purple pop eye looked up at Mrs. Zookey.

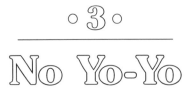

∘ 3 ∘
No Yo-Yo

It could have been a floor monster. Both halves of an eyeball sat on the green tile at the tips of Mrs. Zookey's shoes.

The floor monster looked funny but nobody laughed. Nobody laughed until Mrs. Zookey did.

She laughed and shook her head. "A flying eye," she said. "I thought I'd seen everything, but I've never seen split eyes before. Whose are they?"

Most kids didn't know. They'd been looking at the flag.

We knew at Table Two, but we didn't tell.

I couldn't look at Mrs. Zookey. Neither could

Ben. He stared down at the empty string that hung loose from his finger.

A couple of kids saw the string and pointed, but I think Mrs. Zookey already knew.

"They're mine," Ben said. "They used to be mine."

"They still are," she told him. "You can put the parts on my desk. I think some of you are holding whole ones. Before we get a bonked head or a cracked window, I'd like you to place all your yo-yos on my desk where we can keep an eye on them."

I was sure everybody but me had one, but they didn't. Besides Ben's, only seven eyeballs were lined up on Mrs. Zookey's desk.

When I asked Dawn Marie where hers was, she made a pig nose at me.

"I used to spin a pretty mean yo-yo myself," Mrs. Zookey told us. "Mine never looked like eyes or baseballs or lemons, though. Mine were always just plain yo-yos. I tell you what, I'll bring one of my old yo-yos to school tomorrow. At recess time, those of you who have them can show your tricks, and I'll do one called Rock the Baby. Anybody know that?"

Ben sat down. His bottom lip got big and it began to shake.

"I'll bring along a couple of extras for those of you who don't have one," she said, looking at Ben. "All I have are the plain ones. Because of their shapes, I think they might even work a little better."

Ben sniffed, but he didn't cry.

"It's time for Lunch Count," Yolanda said very loud.

"What's for lunch?" somebody asked.

"Rubber dogs and booger burgers," Michael called from Table One.

All the kids laughed.

Yolanda frowned. Still using her superloud Teacher's Pet voice, she said, "Chicken Licken sandwiches. That's what's on the menu. Everybody who wants it hold up your hand."

Yolanda counted and wrote down the number.

"OK, everybody who wants milk hold up your hand. Higher," she said. "I can't tell if you want milk or you're just scratching your heads."

Then we went on to Yummies and Yuckies.

After Lunch Count we always have Yummies and Yuckies. You get to stand up and talk about something that's happened to you. It's like Show and Tell, only you have to say whether you like it (that's a Yummy) or whether it's gross (that's a Yucky).

Ben could have told a Yucky about how his yo-yo broke, but everybody already knew.

One kid had made the winning goal in a soccer game. That was a Yummy.

Dawn Marie had gone to a movie that was part Yummy and part Yucky. "I give it two and a half stars," she said.

"I've got a Yucky," Michael said. "My little sister's got cooties."

"I like that game," Linda said. "It's not a Yucky at all."

"It is so," Michael told her. "My sister's cooties aren't a game. They're bugs, little teeny tiny bugs that hang onto her hair and don't want to come out. They're the yuckiest."

"Most people call them head lice," Mrs. Zookey explained, "and it's true, they are very small bugs that are a very big nuisance. If you have to choose between Yummies and Yuckies, they definitely fit the Yucky category."

Then she turned and unrolled a big map behind her. It hung down like a window shade.

"But now, my friends," she went on, "we're going from tiny animals who live on heads to very big creatures who live on the land. Some of these you have seen at the zoo. When they live free, they live here." She pointed to the map. "This," she told us, "is Africa."

∘ 4 ∘

It's a Secret

"Richard," Mrs. Zookey said, "your plate is empty."

It was art time and every table was doing a different African animal. Table Two was making lion heads out of paper plates.

You had to draw the lion's face on your plate. I hadn't made a face. My plate didn't look like it should have a face on it. It looked like it should have a hot dog and baked beans. And a pickle.

Ben took a yellow crayon from the can on the table. He gave his lion long sharp teeth.

Linda's lion was wearing lipstick. Dawn Marie's had lots of eyelashes. The girls were already curling batches of orange paper strips around their pencils. You had to paste these on to make the lions' manes.

I grabbed a red crayon. There was lots of stuff to do. First you made the animal head. Then you had to write an animal poem. That was the project.

"You're off to a good start," Mrs. Zookey told us and went on to Table Three. They got to do zebras.

Dawn Marie took a bow from her hair. It was made of so many loops of ribbon it looked like a green octopus. She stuck it on Linda's lion.

Linda took it off the lion, put it in her hair, and tilted her head. "What do you think?" she asked.

"I think it would look better *here*," Dawn Marie said. She leaned over, grabbed the bow, and stuck it on top of Ben's head. The ribbons hung down over his eyes.

"Pretty Benny. Pretty Benny," Dawn Marie sang.

"Pretty Benny. Pretty Benny," we all went. Except Ben.

He shook the bow out of his hair, picked it up, and flew it to the top of my head.

"This thing feels like a bird's nest," I told Dawn Marie. "How do you wear stuff like that all day?"

She grabbed it and set it on the crayon can like it was a flower. "I got it for my birthday, and it's beautiful. It's a lot better than a silly yo-yo."

"Hey, Richard," Ben said, poking me with his elbow. "You want to hear something really gross?"

"How gross?" I asked him, giving my lion a black eye.

Dawn Marie and Linda looked up from their glue and scissors. Dawn Marie made a pig nose at him.

"Grosser than . . . girls," he told us.

"Nothing's that gross," I said.

He cupped his hands and whispered something in my ear.

I went, "Yuck!" His whisper was so wet I had to wipe my ear with my sleeve. Besides, he smelled funny. I couldn't figure out what he smelled like, but he smelled funny. "Yuck," I said again.

"I told you it was gross," he said.

My ear was still wet. I wasn't even sure what he'd said. It sounded like "Pumpkin's got headlights." Did he mean a jack-o'-lantern had a candle in it? What was gross about that? I didn't know what he was talking about, but I stuck out my tongue, crossed my eyes, and held my nose anyway.

Dawn Marie and Linda laughed. So did Ben.

He put his lion head in front of his face and growled.

"It's a pig!" he went. "It's a plane! It's Superlion! Grrrrrrrr."

"Grrrrrrrr!" we growled with him. All four of us growled together.

Mrs. Zookey raised her head.

"Grrrrrrrr," we went again. This time we did it with our lips shut so she couldn't tell it was us.

Mrs. Zookey walked our direction. She could tell.

"Table Two," she said, "I think I hear your stomachs growling. They'll have to wait. Lunch isn't for an hour."

Everybody around us laughed. Kids laugh in Mrs. Zookey's room. That's OK. You just can't talk too loud or act too weird.

"Grrrrrrr," we went, to make them laugh again.

"All right, Table Two," Mrs. Zookey said. "You're louder than too loud. Stick to your projects."

Dawn Marie smiled. She squeezed the glue bottle until a wiggly white snake of glue oozed out onto her lion's paper head.

"It's alive. It's alive," she whispered. She wiped the hair out of her eyes with her sleeve and then she squeezed some more. But then, instead of pressing paper curls on the thick, white goo, she stuck her *hand* in it.

Linda gasped. "You're going to get it, Dawn Marie," she said. "You're really going to get it."

Dawn Marie waved the plate at us. It hung on her hand like a tack on a magnet. "Mrs. Zookey said stick to your project," she whispered. "I only did what she *said*."

We laughed out loud again. We couldn't help it.

Mrs. Zookey did not laugh. "Table Two," she told us, "you were supposed to be first in all the lines today. Now you will have to be last. You are not sticking to your projects."

We stopped laughing. Being last in line for lunch and recess is no fun.

Dawn Marie hid her sticky hand so Mrs. Zookey wouldn't know.

"What I told you is a secret," Ben said quietly. "Don't you tell."

That was easy. It wasn't even Halloween. Who

would care about a pumpkin with headlights?

"Can you guess who it is?"

I shook my head.

"I'll give you a clue," he went on. "It's somebody in our class."

There wasn't a kid in the room who looked like a pumpkin. Or even a jack-o'-lantern. Dawn Marie had a missing front tooth and new glasses. Maybe he meant Dawn Marie's glasses.

"Dawn Marie is wearing headlights," I sang loud enough that she could hear but Mrs. Zookey couldn't.

Dawn Marie peeled the paper plate off her hand, reached across the table, and wiped a fat gob of glue on my shirt.

"I am rubber," Dawn Marie said. "You are glue. What you say bounces off me and sticks to you."

"So there," Linda told me.

My arm was cold and sticky. Even though she was Table Two I wanted to tell on Dawn Marie.

Ben pulled my sleeve around to look at the mess. The glue was thick and white and yucky. And something was in it. I had to look close to see what it was.

In the middle of the smear of goo a tiny gray bug was trying to swim.

Flint Lake
Media Center

∘ 5 ∘

Not Me

"A bug bounced off you and stuck to me," I told Dawn Marie.

"It's not my bug," she said. "You can have it." She got up and went to the sink to wash her hands.

"Headlights," Ben said. Sometimes Ben is weird.

"My mom won't like what Dawn Marie did to my shirt," I told him. "It's almost new."

"If that bug is yours, your mom won't like that either." Ben stuck two fingers through his hair and wiggled them like bug feelers.

"Mrs. Zookey," Linda called, "I'm finished." She held up her plate for everyone to see. The front around the face and the whole back of it were covered with orange curls. "I'm ready to start on my poem now," she told us. "Lion, lion, lying on the ground . . ."

Mrs. Zookey took the lion head. She hung it with two elephants on a clothesline that ran the length of the room. On her desk, the yo-yo eyes stared up at them.

I gave my lion a gray frown and stuck a thumb on my gluey sleeve. There was not one bug in the white stuff. There were two.

"My mom won't mind them," I told Ben. "They're little. She's not scared of bugs."

"She'll hate those," he said. "For sure."

I took a deep breath. I smelled like white glue.

"You know what that bug is, don't you?" Ben asked me, talking low so nobody else could hear. "That's what I told you was a secret."

"You told me, 'Pumpkin's got headlights.'"

"I told you," he said, "'Some kid's got head lice.'"

"Pumpkin's," I said again, "got headlights. I like that a whole lot better."

"Head lice?" Linda asked. She'd been listening. She scooted her chair away from the table. "Has Richard got head lice?"

"Not me," I said. "I don't know what those bugs are. Maybe they're paste bugs."

"I know about head lice," Linda told us. "My sister said they grow inside your head and crawl out your ears."

"That's a lie," Ben told her. "They grow in eggs that get all stuck in your hair. The eggs are white and they're called nits."

"How come you know so much?" I asked him.

"My mom said they were going around," Linda told us. "She said not to get them."

I curled some paper strips around my pencil and let them spring off onto the table.

"These aren't lice," I said. "These are just plain bugs."

"There's no such thing as just plain bugs," Linda told me. "They've got to have names like ant and bee and mosquito."

"I can't tell what they are," I said, staring down at the bugs stuck in glue. "But they're too little to be ants or bees or mosquitoes."

Ben made little gray dots on his lion's curls.

"Lice," he said, "have got drills in their mouths. They drill teeny tiny holes in your skin." He grinned at us so we couldn't tell if he was lying or not.

"That's a lie," Linda said.

"No lie," Ben told her. "They drill holes. Then they suck out blood. There are lots of them. One is called a louse. Lots of them are lice. Like mouse and mice." He was dotting his lion's head full of bugs.

"That's sick," I said.

"Anyway," he went on, making his voice all low like he was telling a monster story. "Anyway, after this louse drills a hole and sucks out blood, guess what it does?"

We didn't guess.

"It *spits* in the hole."

"Spits?" I stuck my finger down my throat like I could throw up.

"I'm going to tell Mrs. Zookey," Linda said. She started to raise her hand, but she didn't.

"And the spit," Ben kept going, "makes your head itch. It makes it itch a lot."

"A bug can't spit. That's a lie for sure," I told him.

"Is not a lie. It's true."

"If it *is* true, how come you know so much?" I asked him again.

Dawn Marie sat back down at the table with clean hands. Linda whispered to her.

"Lice!" Dawn Marie said, and they pointed at the bugs on my sleeve and laughed.

I couldn't get rid of the bugs without smearing the glue all over. They weren't moving. I think they were dead.

Linda began to hum "London Bridge Is Falling Down."

Dawn Marie started to sing it as she pasted curls around her paper plate. But she didn't use the right words. She sang, "Richard's head is full of bugs, full of bugs, full of bugs. . . ."

Linda sang with her. "Richard's head is full of bugs. . . ."

And Ben put in the last line. "He's got cooties."

∘ 6 ∘

Baby, Baby

"Your lion is bald," Ben told me. It was, too. All the paper curls at our table had been used up.

"I don't care." I drew two orange ears on the plate. "It's a mother lion," I told him. "They don't have manes."

I hadn't written my poem yet. It was ten minutes to bell time.

And my head itched. It itched like a billion bugs had drilled holes in my skin and spit in them. I couldn't scratch. I wouldn't let the rest of Table Two see me scratch. If I did they would start to sing, "Richard's head is full of bugs," all over again.

"OK, listen," Linda said. "Here's my poem." She read it off her sheet of paper.

> "Lion, lion,
>   Lying on the ice.
>   Your tail is black.
>   Your head's got . . . guess what."

"*Lice*," Dawn Marie and Ben said together.

"Right, Richard?" Linda asked.

"There isn't any ice where lions live," I said. "That's no good." I sat on my hands to keep from scratching.

"You want to hear mine?" Dawn Marie asked.

> "Noses are red,
>   Cats like mice.
>   The lion is itchy
>   Because his hair has got . . ."

"*Lice*." Ben and Linda finished it.

"That's no good, either," I said. "It's not really a lion poem."

"Here's mine," Ben told us.

> "Lion, lion,
>   Jumped up twice . . ."

"That's enough," I said. "I don't care. Your stupid lions may have lice, but I don't."

I chewed on my pencil and tried to decide what to write. The rest of Table Two turned in their no-good poems. They sat down and waited for the bell to ring while I worked on my poem. At least I knew what it *wasn't* going to be about.

I wrote and wrote, and when I was through, I put a dot on the paper to show that was the end. "I finished," I said.

"Does anything rhyme with rice?" Dawn Marie asked.

"Cut it out," I told her.

"Aren't you going to read it?" she asked. "We read ours."

"OK," I said. "I'll read it if you won't laugh."

"We won't laugh unless it's funny," she said.

I read it fast.

> "The lion has a roar.
> The lion has a sneeze.
> He eats up baby antelopes.
> At least he doesn't *tease*."

Dawn Marie laughed and pointed at my arm. I reached over and rubbed the bugs and the

glue off my sleeve. That made my hand all sticky. Then my eyes began to sting like I was going to cry. A little water came out of them.

"I'm sorry," Linda said.

My nose was running, so I wiped it on my clean sleeve.

That's when Dawn Marie started to sing,

"Baby, baby,
Stick your head in gravy.
Wash it off with bubble gum
And send it to the navy."

"That wasn't nice," Ben told her. "Richard can't help it if he's got lice. Besides, sticking his head in gravy wouldn't help. Or plain water either. That's because lice can live underwater for two whole days. And nits stick in your hair as bad as bubble gum. I mean it."

"How come you know so much?" I asked him. "How come?"

"Boys and girls," Mrs. Zookey called. "May I have your attention, please. A note has just come from the school nurse. This is important. A case of head lice has been reported in this class."

I looked at Ben. Ben looked at me.

Dawn Marie giggled.

"How did the nurse know so soon?" I asked him. He didn't answer.

"Oh, my," Mrs. Zookey said. "That means that this afternoon the nurse will need to check each of your heads to see if you have them. Then we will spend some time talking about—"

ZZZZZZZINNNNNNNG. The bell rang for lunch.

Table Two was last in line.

"Don't share your baseball caps over the lunch hour," Mrs. Zookey said as we filed out. "Don't share your combs. Don't share your coats. If those little bugs brush off one place they catch onto a new one."

Chicken Licken sandwiches are my favorite cafeteria lunch. I wasn't hungry.

The kids at my table were all talking about lice and how you get them. Some kids said they only got in long hair.

That was good. I don't have long hair.

One kid said they dropped on you from trees.

That was bad. I walk under lots of trees.

Some kids said you got them from dogs.

I hoped my dog Ted didn't have them.

Ben didn't eat with me. He ate with Michael. I listened to them laugh a lot. I just knew they were laughing at me.

○ 7 ○

To the Nurse, to the Nurse, to the Nurse, Nurse, Nurse

When we got back from lunch, there was a picture on the board. Mrs. Zookey had drawn it with yellow chalk. It was a bug with a big body and a little head. It had six hairy legs with hooks at the ends. The yo-yo eyeballs lined up across Mrs. Zookey's desk were staring at it.

The bug on the board was as big as a football, but I could guess what it was.

"Remember the magnifying lens?" Mrs. Zookey asked us. She held up this glass we'd looked through once. It had made little grains of salt look like big boxes. "If you looked through this magnifying lens at a louse, this is pretty much what you'd see." She pointed to the picture.

Everybody went, "Eeuuuuu gross."

"They aren't really bad," she said. "They're just bugs. They don't make you sick, but they aren't any fun to have on your head. If you have them, you have to get rid of them."

Michael wrapped his arms around his head. "I see one flying though the air right now. I'm getting out of here." He stood up. I don't know where he thought he was going to go.

"Do you see any wings on this bug?" Mrs. Zookey asked, pointing to her picture on the board.

I didn't see any wings.

Michael didn't see any either. "You forgot them," he told her.

"I didn't forget," she said. "Lice don't have wings. They can't fly. They can't even jump. They go from head to head only if you touch heads."

Dawn Marie held up her hand. "Ben says they

drill holes in your skin and suck your blood. That's not true," she said. She stuck out her tongue at Ben.

"Actually," Mrs. Zookey said, "that *is* true. They do feed off people's heads."

Everybody went, "Eeuuuuu gross," again.

"Do the eggs really stick in your head like bubble gum?" I asked her.

"Yes," she told me, "I'm afraid they do."

"I don't have them," one kid said.

"Maybe," Mrs. Zookey told her. "Maybe not. Each of you will go to the nurse to find out."

"Do we have to?" Dawn Marie asked.

"Yes," Mrs. Zookey said. "You have to. Table Three will be first."

That was good. Some lines you don't want to be first in.

"I'd die if I had them. I'd be so embarrassed I'd just *die*," Linda said.

"No," Mrs. Zookey told her. "You'd wash your head with a special shampoo and *they* would die. All of you, listen, now. You don't have to be embarrassed if you have lice. Anybody can get them. The lice don't care where they land. You just have to have a nice warm head."

A kid with a new haircut raised his hand. "You have to have long hair," he said.

"Not true," Mrs. Zookey told him. "Long or short, the lice don't care."

"I hear they drop on your head from trees," Michael said.

"Not true," Mrs. Zookey told him. "Trees sometimes have a kind of lice called aphids, but aphids don't live on people."

"You can get them from dogs," a kid at Table Four said.

"Not true," Mrs. Zookey told us. "Dogs sometimes get lice, but they are dog lice. People only get lice that have lived on other people. But," she went on, "these lice can live on beds or rugs or sofas or chairs, away from people's heads, for about ten days. That's why—if you have lice—your clothing at home will have to be washed. So will your sheets and blankets. And your rugs and furniture will need spraying. These are pesky bugs, hard to get rid of."

Ben raised his hand. "You want to know how they get born? I know how they get born. My dad told me. He's a doctor and he knows."

"How come he told you about lice?" I asked Ben, but he didn't say. He just kept talking.

"My dad says that unless you stop her, the mother louse lays about three or four eggs a day in your hair for about a month."

Everybody was scratching his head. Or her head. I mean, you couldn't help it. Just talking about bugs stuck on your head makes you itch.

"This is funny," Ben said. "I remember it because it's very funny. The egg just sits there being sticky for about a week, and then the baby bug inside pokes a hole in the end of the egg. But the hole isn't big enough for the baby bug to get out. So the baby bug sticks its little head through the hole and takes a big breath. He lets go and shoots the air out to the back of the egg. But it's not enough air. So he just keeps doing it. He takes another breath and shoots it back. Finally he does it enough so that he just pops out of the egg like a jet. And that's how a louse gets born and starts to crawl around your head. Isn't that funny?"

By now even Mrs. Zookey was scratching her head.

"How come your dad told you that?" I asked.

He made a face.

"You weren't home practicing yo-yo tricks yesterday at all, were you?" I asked him.

Ben made his voice low. "My dad told me all

that stuff Saturday while he was washing my head with Lice-Kill shampoo. He picked sticky nits out of my hair last night. He and Mom took turns. I watched TV. They picked my nits until they were all gone. The nurse checked my head when I came back to school this morning."

"Table Three," Mrs. Zookey said, "the nurse is expecting you."

I bet Table Three was sorry they'd been good all day. Everybody stared at them. As soon as they left, I turned to Ben. "Are you the pumpkin with headlights?" I asked him.

"That's me," he said. "My head was a jungle."

Mrs. Zookey sat on her desk next to the eyeball yo-yos. She picked up Linda's orange one. "May I try?" she asked Linda.

Linda said yes, so Mrs. Zookey put the string loop around her finger and curled her hand up over the yo-yo. She held it that way for a minute and then she opened her fingers. The yo-yo rolled out of her hand and fell toward the floor. The orange eye rolled down without blinking. Then it stopped, just like Ben's had when I tried it.

She's no good at this, I thought. She said she was. But she's no good at all. She's just a teacher.

And then the yo-yo snapped back up into her hand. "When it just sits at the bottom for awhile, that's called Sleeping," she said. "I'll show you how tomorrow."

She did know yo-yos. But maybe I'd never learn them. If I had lice I wouldn't be at recess tomorrow. And I had lice. I could feel their drills. I looked at the picture on the chalkboard. It had a mean face.

"Let's see," Mrs. Zookey said, putting the yo-yo back with the others. "While we wait for everyone to visit the nurse, I'll read a story." She picked up a book. "I'll make it one that's far, far removed from sticky hair. I'll read you a book about lions that roam the hilly plains of central Africa."

We listened and scratched our heads.

∘ 8 ∘
Do I?

Being last in line wasn't all that good. We had to wait a long time. The nurse must have checked every hair on every kid's head. While we waited Mrs. Zookey read a whole stack of stories about lions and elephants and zebras. She sang us a song about a gnu. I didn't think much about the lions and elephants and zebras. Or even about the gnu. I thought about the big, fat louse on the chalkboard.

Finally, Mrs. Zookey nodded to Table Two.

I knew I had them. I just knew it. Baby lice were jumping rope in my hair. They were playing hide and seek. I could feel them.

Linda, Dawn Marie, Ben, and I went straight to

the nurse's office. Even though nobody was in the hall to see us, we didn't do a single thing we weren't supposed to do. We didn't stick our thumbs on the water fountain to squirt the ceiling. We didn't race each other to the gym door. We didn't even talk.

Outside the nurse's office, we sat on chairs and waited for her to call our names. I crossed my hands in my lap. Maybe if I was good the lice would go away.

Mrs. Graff, the nurse, looked around the corner.

"Ben," she said, "I've already seen you today, but I'll give you a quick once-over anyway." Ben left and we each moved down one seat.

Dawn Marie poked me with her elbow. She started humming "London Bridge," but I knew what words she was singing in her head. I didn't look at her.

When Ben came out of the nurse's office, he was grinning. "No nits is good nits," he said.

"Richard," Mrs. Graff called.

"Will it hurt?" I asked her when I walked in.

"I'm just going to look," she said. "Take a seat."

I sat. She swung a wall lamp over my head. It lit up a magnifying lens as big as a saucer.

Mrs. Graff put the light and the glass over my head to make everything look big. Then with her fingers she went on a monster hunt.

"Do I have them?" I asked her. "Do I have them?"

She pushed my hair from side to side.

"Do I?"

She turned the light off and moved the magnifying glass away. "I found something," she said.

I knew it. I'd known it all along. I had a lice farm.

"Behind your ears," she said. "You've started two small mountain ranges of dirt. I'd go at them with a washcloth tonight if I were you."

"No Lice-Kill shampoo?"

"No need," she said. "No lice. But remember—"

"No sharing caps," I told her.

I ran from the office and nobody stopped me. I waved at Linda and Dawn Marie and skipped down the hall. On the way I stopped at the drinking fountain. I turned it on, covered the hole with my thumb, and sprayed my face wet.

Little drops of water ran down my face as I sang, all the way back to the room, "Richard hasn't got a bug, got a bug, got a bug. . . ."

○ 9 ○

She's Got Cooties

When Linda came back, she said, "I don't have them, but Dawn Marie does. The nurse made her go home. She's got to wash her hair with Lice-Kill shampoo."

They were Dawn Marie's lice. Those bugs on the glue were Dawn Marie's all the time.

"Did she catch them from *you*?" I asked Ben.

He stretched his mouth wide and stuck his tongue out. "You know what else," he told me. "She'll have to wash her head with vinegar to get the sticky nits loose."

"She'll smell like you," I said.

"Do I smell?"

"You smell like salad dressing," I told him. I'd finally figured it out.

"I may smell but I don't itch anymore. Michael does, I bet. He has them. Three kids have them, not counting me because mine are gone," Ben whispered.

"Bummer," I said.

"Six spelling words are on the board," Mrs. Zookey said. "They are the names of all the animals you made to hang on our clothesline. They are all animals who live in Africa. Copy the words neatly."

While we were writing *zebra* and *gnu*, Mrs. Zookey came over to talk to us.

"Dawn Marie does have head lice," she told us, "so you all must be very careful. Remember, no sharing . . ."

"Coats," Linda said.

"Caps," I told her.

"Combs," Ben added.

"And ribbons, too, of course," Mrs. Zookey said. She reached over and picked up the green octopus bow that sat on top of the crayon can. "This is Dawn Marie's, isn't it?" she asked.

Linda nodded and scratched her head.

We all three moved our seats back as if the bow would reach out and bite us.

"I'll give it to her mother," Mrs. Zookey said. "She can tie it up in a plastic bag for a month, and that will kill any lice that may be on the ribbons. It's much too pretty to throw away."

Ben looked at me. I looked at Ben. We had both had Dawn Marie's bow on our heads.

What if one louse, one silly louse, had ridden on it from her head to Linda's to Ben's to mine? What if that's where it got off? What if that one tiny bug was too little for the nurse to see? What if it was up there right now laying sticky eggs in my hair? My head began to itch again.

"Oh, dear," Linda said. "Oh, dear."

"Let's just forget about it for a while," Mrs. Zookey told her. She gave Linda a small hug.

When Mrs. Zookey leaned down, her big silver earrings clicked. I looked at them. I looked at Mrs. Zookey. Then I looked at Ben.

"What's wrong?" Ben asked.

Mrs. Zookey smiled and went away.

"Nothing," I said.

"Do you think we all got them from the bow?" Linda asked.

Table Two likes doing some things together, but not raising lice.

"I've got a secret," I told them.

"What is it?" Linda whispered.

The kids at the other tables were all busy writing down animal words.

"Mrs. Zookey won't bring her yo-yos to school tomorrow," I whispered back. "She won't show us how a yo-yo Sleeps or how to Rock the Baby."

"Why not?" Ben asked. "I'm going to show everybody how to Walk the Dog. I can do that one really good."

"Mrs. Zookey's going to be absent tomorrow," I told him.

"How do *you* know?" Linda asked.

"Table Two," Mrs. Zookey called from her desk. "You have work to do that you can't do when you're talking."

We wrote down more spelling words—*lion, hippopotamus*. We were quiet. We were quiet for five minutes.

"How do you know she'll be absent?" Ben asked me.

"She's got bugs," I said.

"Bugs?"

"Bugs. I saw two near her ear. I bet I know what kind of bugs they are."

Linda leaned toward me. "Mrs. Zookey can't have lice," she said. "She's a teacher."

"That doesn't matter," I told her. "Mrs. Zookey said that all you need is a good warm head."

"She could have got them from hugging some kid," Ben said.

"Tomorrow," I told him, "she'll be washing pillows and sheets. . . ."

"And caps and dresses . . ." Linda went on.

"And hair," Ben said. "And hair."

"Almost bell time," Mrs. Zookey announced. "I promise you we'll have a calmer day tomorrow. Remember to bring your yo-yo for recess tomorrow, if you have one. If you don't have one, you're welcome to borrow one of mine. Tomorrow we'll be back to normal."

"She doesn't know yet," I told Table Two.

"We don't have to tell her, do we?" Linda asked.

"She'll find out," Ben said.

ZZZZZZZINNNNNNNG. The bell rang.

Table Two was the last to go.

On their way out, kids took their eyeball yo-yos off of Mrs. Zookey's desk.

Ben picked up both parts of his. He gave me the eye half. "For good luck," he said.

The eye stared up at me from my hand.

"It's excellent," I told him. "But I don't think I'll get one."

"Plain yo-yos are best," he said, and I agreed.

"I'll see you tomorrow," Mrs. Zookey told us.

What if she doesn't find out, I wondered.

"Mrs. Zookey," I said.

Ben and Linda stopped and stared at me.

"Mrs. Zookey?" I asked.

"Yes, Richard," Mrs. Zookey said.

"Mrs. Zookey, is it true that you don't have to be embarrassed if you've got lice?"

"It's true, Richard," Mrs. Zookey said. "Don't you worry."

"Is it true that all you have to do is wash your hair with special shampoo and it will kill them dead?" I asked her.

"It's true, Richard," she said. "We know what to do about them."

"Mrs. Zookey," I tried again, "do we have to feel sorry for people who get lice?"

"Certainly not," she said. "Dawn Marie will be back in a day or so."

I looked at Ben and Linda. They looked at the ceiling. They weren't going to help. I wasn't sure I could do it.

"Mrs. Zookey," I went on, "are you going to have a head check, too?"

"Why, I hadn't thought of it," she said. "But that might not be a bad idea. I've never actually seen how the nurse does it." She didn't seem worried at all. "Thank you, Richard."

She'd find out all right.

We hurried into the hall.

"I thought you were going to tell her." Linda spun her yo-yo up and down.

"I tried," I said. "I wanted to, but I just couldn't say she had bugs."

"When she finds out," Ben told me, "she'll know you saw them. She'll know."

He started to hum. By the time we got to the water fountain he was singing, "Mrs. Zookey's got a bug, got a bug, got a bug. . . ."

Linda pumped her yo-yo and she sang, too. "Got a bug, got a bug . . ."

All those lice were drilling Mrs. Zookey's head.

Way behind us, I could hear her heels clicking down the hall.

I turned and ran back to where she was. She'd said we didn't have to feel sorry, but I did.

She stopped. "Richard," she said, "what's wrong?"

Reaching out, I handed her my half of the purple eyeball yo-yo. "This is for luck," I said. "I really hope you have a nice day at home tomorrow."

She took the purple eye. "At home," she said, and she put her hand on top of her red hair.

I nodded and hurried back to Ben and Linda. Even before I got there I could hear them still singing the song.

"Mrs. Zookey's got a buuuuuuug."

We all three scratched our heads.

"She's got cooties."

About the Author

Author of eleven previous novels, including *Do Bananas Chew Gum?* and the popular group of books featuring Hobie Hanson, Jamie Gilson writes about funny things that happen to children in the Midwest, where she has always lived. A graduate of Northwestern University's speech school, she taught junior high school for one year, wrote and directed educational radio and television programs for the Chicago public schools, wrote commercials for fine arts radio station WFMT, and wrote films and filmstrips for Encyclopedia Britannica Films. For ten years she was a columnist for *Chicago* magazine. She and her husband live in a suburb of Chicago. They have three amazing children.

Jamie Gilson has never had lice, but she scratched her head a lot while writing this book.